CUFFED TO A SAVAGE 2

LOVING A SAVAGE BOOK 2

MIA BLACK

CHAPTER 1

I WAS SITTING CLOSE to Young and I couldn't help but think about how everything felt different. It didn't feel like we were us. I didn't feel like Taela at all. *Taela* was more responsible than this situation so I wasn't sure of who I was at the moment. I tried not to let it happen but thoughts of my mother snuck into my head and I couldn't even help but to think what she would say. It didn't matter how the situation turned out, she'd *definitely* have a word or two to throw in.

Young and I were sitting across from one another at his dining table. We couldn't have been more than a few feet apart but it felt like we were in two different worlds. Neither of us were talking. We hadn't spoken in a few minutes. We weren't looking at one another either. I didn't want to say anything. There was a lot that could have been said but it was probably best for us to just stay quiet.

The situation that we were in was crazy. I'd just taken a home pregnancy test and we were waiting for the results. I had been having sex since I was 17 years old and I'd never had a pregnancy scare before. I was always safe and careful so my little slip up with Young had been pretty out of character for me. I'd been so caught up in the moment that it wasn't even a thought to put on a condom. I was on the pill but I forgot to take it sometimes. I didn't feel too pressed to do it because it had been so long since I'd had sex.

I didn't know what was going through Young's mind but all that was going through mine was what would happen if the test came back positive. I couldn't even begin to imagine what it would be like. I couldn't be a mother. I was still way too young. I still hadn't traveled the world and stuff. I didn't have any money saved or anything. I knew that I could still do all the things I wanted to do but I was still young and I could admit that I wanted to be selfish for a couple more years.

I was also facing the realization that if I was pregnant and had the baby, I'd have to co-parent with Young. We'd only known one another for two weeks and still had a long way to go before we became a couple, let alone parents. I never wanted to be a baby mama but I also didn't think that the two of us trying to force ourselves into a relationship for the next nine months for the sake of the baby was the right thing to do. I was getting ahead of myself though because nothing had been confirmed.

My phone snapped me from my thoughts as the timer I set went off. I'd set it right after I took the test. I needed to know the exact second that it was ready. I was going to put the test on the table but I'd left it on the counter over in the kitchen. I knew that if it was right in front of us that we wouldn't have done anything besides just stare at it.

I got up and walked over to the counter where the test was, reading the directions on the back for what had to have been the 50th time. I knew them like they were a speech I needed to memorize back in high school. I made sure to call Young and tell him to get one of the simpler tests. I didn't have time to be guessing colors and stuff like that. If there were two lines then I was pregnant, one line meant that I wasn't.

I closed my eyes and said a quick prayer. The funny thing was that I didn't know what I was praying for. Being pregnant was a blessing, even if I wasn't ready. I think I just wanted strength. I took a deep breath and opened them. "Negative!" I said loudly. I turned my head to Young.

I didn't even realize it but I'd been holding my breath. I exhaled slowly and let myself feel a little bit of happiness about the results. It felt like I was breathing new life, no pun intended. I was relieved. I turned around to Young and it looked like he had the same look on his face. I went back over to the table and sat down across from him.

"That was scary," I said.

"Hell yeah," he agreed. He looked a lot more relaxed now. I wondered what had gone through his head. "We can't slip up no more."

"I know," I said. "It was our first time but we can't let it happen again." He nodded his head in agreement.

"What were you gonna do if it came back positive?" Young asked. He had a look of genuine curiosity on his face.

I shook my head a little bit. I didn't even want to think about it but I did know how I felt about pregnancy in general. "I think that in situations like that this it's best to just leave it up to the woman. It's her body." I didn't know what would have happened with the pregnancy but I think that while I would have spoken to Young about it a lot, ultimately it would have been my decision.

Young's face didn't change much. "If it would've come back positive, I get that you have a choice but you know what the right choice is." He still had the same serious expression on his face.

I was shocked, so much so that it took me a couple of seconds to recover. I screwed my face up and looked at him. I didn't expect for Young to be pro-life and I *definitely* didn't expect him to want me to have his baby, especially not so soon. We barely knew one another. "Why?" I asked. That was as far as I could get. I just needed to hear his explanation.

"I just feel like stuff like that happens for a

reason," he said. "I get what you mean about your body and your choice and all that but it's not only your choice. The baby would've been half mine." He'd raised his voice a little bit in a warning tone of voice.

I really couldn't believe what I was hearing. I was about to open my mouth and give him a quick education on *why* I had a choice but I decided not to. I had to stop and look at the fact that we were having our first real disagreement and it was over such a big topic. We were only two weeks into whatever this was going to turn into.

"Let's just drop this," I said. I was definitely trying to avoid an argument.

Young must have thought I was trying to use some reverse psychology on him or something like that because he looked a little confused.

"I was just thinking that this is the first time we've kind of argued about something. This is a big ass topic to try and talk about right now," I explained. "If we gonna argue then it should be over something small like your feet stinking."

He nodded his head and smiled a little at my joke. "I know what you mean. It's a whole bunch of other shit we should know about each other before we get to this like this. I think we should take it as a warning though. We just gotta be aware of stuff going forward," he said.

"We do," I said. I wanted to lighten the conversation. "So, are we gonna eat this Chipotle or what?"

Young and I sat at the table and ate the food he'd brought. We talked, chatting with one another like normal and putting all of that pregnancy scare stuff behind us. I left after we finished eating. I needed to get back to my house so I could start getting ready for the work week ahead of me.

I was still all incognito when I left Young's apartment. I was dressed in a hat, sunglasses and a long cardigan. It was a nice disguise and unless you got all into my face, I was pretty discreet.

It was a nice day outside so I decided to walk home. It would probably talk me almost an hour but I didn't mind. The long walk would give me time to think about things. I was still thinking about dating Young and what it meant. We were from two opposite worlds. The problem was that if our worlds collided, it wouldn't be a good thing.

The longer I walked, the more the other side of my brain started to speak up more. It might have been scandalous and all but the feeling of excitement that I was getting from it was amazing. Not to mention that I could really see myself and Young going somewhere in the long run. I wanted to see it through and the only way to do that would be by continuing to see him. I knew that I was potentially putting my job on the line but it just meant that we'd both need to be careful.

All of the walking and thinking that I'd been doing made me tired. I was close to my apartment building, only about a block away or so, when I decided to stop at the bodega on the corner to get an apple juice. I'd definitely gotten a thirst over the course of the long walk.

The store was brightly lit and well stocked. I'd go in there every now and then to grab something. They didn't make sandwiches though so I didn't go too often. The store was long kind of narrow. Against one wall was a fridge that held an assortment of drinks. In the middle was a big shelf that made and aisle. At the front of the store was the counter.

I grabbed an apple juice from the fridge and

headed to the counter to pay for it. Normally I'd just throw my money on the counter and hold up my item before I walked out but there was a little crowd in front of it.

A woman had two kids, a boy and a girl, with her and was holding everyone up because her food stamp card wasn't working properly. While waiting for her card to work, the guy behind the counter was talking numbers from this old lady who was just rattling off numbers to him so fast that I was surprised he could even keep up with her. Behind them, some college kid was buying a six pack. I studied his face for a little bit and judged that he was 21. I hoped the guy behind the counter carded him.

I knew that I was the one who chose to walk and stuff but I wasn't trying to be outside for any longer than I had to be. I definitely wasn't trying to wait, especially not when there was another store down the block that I could get juice *and* a sandwich from. I turned around and was about to walk back down the aisle to put the juice back when a booming voice behind me startled me.

"Everybody get the fuck down, now!" the voice yelled. It snapped me from my thoughts. I dropped the juice in my hand and it hit the floor with a small bounce and thud.

A guy wearing a black hoodie and jeans had just burst into the store. Literally in the few second that it took me to turn around he'd come in. He had a gun in his hand and was waving it around. He pointed it at the man behind the counter and then waved it around at everyone.

I couldn't believe what was happening. The guy behind the counter looked shocked. The mother instinctively pulled her kids behind her. She backed up a couple of feet, almost tripping over them.

"Oh my God!" the old woman yelled. She dropped the lottery tickets she was holding and they floated to the ground.

"What the fuck?" the college aged guy said. He was clutching the beer in his hand tightly to his chest. I was afraid a can might burst or something.

"Stay behind me!" the mother yelled at her kids. She was trying to use her body to shield them as best she could. The boy was trying to be brave and stand in front of his mother but she was trying to keep him out of the way.

"I said get the fuck down!" he yelled. He

waved the gun around, this time pointing it right into the face of the college guy. He took a couple of steps back and dropped the beers as he backed into a shelf.

"Chill, chill," he pleaded as he got down on the floor.

I ducked down and was glad that everyone else did the same. The energy that this guy was giving was crazy and volatile. He was probably high or something. One wrong move and something bad could happen. I needed to make sure that I was paying attention.

I was afraid. I couldn't front like I wasn't. The fear that I had inside of me wasn't going to stop me. I was going to use the training that I had. I had my service weapon on me but I hoped that I wouldn't have to use it. I hadn't fired it yet and didn't want this to be the first time that I did. I always made sure to have that on me regardless of what disguise or whatever I was wearing.

The would be thief was focused on the cashier now. He'd turned the gun right on him. "Give me all the fucking money!" he demanded. It was almost funny because when I first started I thought it would be just like the TV shows I watched and it wasn't. This situation was definitely something I'd seen on TV but I didn't want to be living it.

"Don't try no funny shit, papi. I'll blow your fucking brains out!" the robber was yelling at the middle aged cashier who was trying his hardest to do as he said. He was moving slowly though, probably in an effort not to get shot.

"I'm going. I'm going," the man said. He pressed some buttons on the register and it sprang to life, popping open.

"Get a fucking bag!" the thief demanded.

Thankfully the guy hadn't turned back around to notice that I was reaching into my coat to grab my gun. The eyes of the other customers weren't really on me. The little boy looked at me and I thought he was about to say something but I shot a look his way and he stopped himself. I was crouching low on one knee but I moved to a squatting position before slowly standing.

I raised the weapon and pointed it square at his back. I didn't want to have to shoot him but if he pushed me...

"NYPD!" I yelled in a voice that was loud

enough to startle him. "Drop the gun and get on the ground, now!"

It worked. I'd managed to surprise him. He turned around quickly with his gun still in hand. He went from startled to outright surprise when he realized that he'd spun around and was now staring at my gun. His eyes scanned my body and landed on my shield that was displayed around my waist.

"Oh shit!" he said. He looked at the gun in my hand and it was like watching a balloon deflate, the way that he was losing his energy,

He dropped his gun to the ground and snatched his hood off his head. He dropped down to his knees. "Please don't shoot. Please! That's not even a loaded gun." He was looking up at me with a pleading look in his eyes. He was obviously afraid that I was going to pull the trigger but he didn't know that I hadn't even taken the safety off.

I felt like I was about to explode. The way that the adrenaline was pumping through my veins had me on fire. I felt so damn powerful. I was surprised that my hands weren't shaking. I had to take charge of the situation. I still had my gun on the would be robber but I turned my head a little bit to speak to the college kid who was still on the floor.

"Do you have a cell phone?" I asked. My eyes were darting back and forth between him and the thief. I didn't think the guy was going to run or anything like that but I wasn't about to chance it anyway.

"Yeah," he said. He was a little dazed but nothing too crazy. It had to be a scary experience for him.

"Call 911," I said. "Let them know you need the police."

I turned to the guy behind the counter. "Do you have a way to lock the door? No one can come in or out until the police get here."

"No problem," the guy said. He had a little Spanish accent. He moved from behind the counter and headed to the door of the store. He locked it and turned back around to me.

"Is there anything else I can do to help?" he asked.

"You've been more than helpful," I said.

I told the woman and her kids that they should move away and I isolated the guy in a corner since I didn't have my handcuffs on me. Once the officers that were called arrived, I turned the situation over to them. I was just a witness, after all.

It was so crazy that I'd had more excitement as a civilian than as an actual officer. Stopping that robbery had been exhilarating. Hours later I still couldn't stop buzzing from the energy of it all. It was funny almost how my day had gone. I'd been on the brink of both near life and near death.

When I believed that there was a chance that I was pregnant, my mind had gone all over. So much stuff had been running through my mind. It was quick but I'd practically lived out my entire life in a few seconds, just by imagining what could have happened. I thought about the ways that my body would change, what I'd be like as a parent, what my kid could look like.

My life hadn't flashed in front of my eyes when the thief bust into the corner store but I had felt more fear than I'd ever felt before. I think that in that moment I really thought about the fact that I could die in the line of duty or, as this situation had proven, outside of it as well. If it hadn't been for my quick thinking, I hated to even wonder where the situation could have gone. The store wasn't crazy packed but a lot of innocent people, including children, could have gotten hurt, and for what? A couple of dollars? I wondered if the guy thought it was worth it. I know that his gun wasn't loaded according to him but what if it had been.

I'd definitely surprised myself when I decided to take action. When I snuck up on the thief, I was prepared to shoot. The entire time that my gun was on him, I was ready...ready for anything. He had a weapon in his hand and that meant that if I would have shot him, it would have been justified. I didn't come into the job wanting or even anticipating anyone's life but I knew that it was a possibility.

When I got home that night I just wanted to chill out. The highs and lows of the day had taken a toll on me. I turned my phone off and decided to take a bubble bath. When I climbed into bed, I said a prayer thanking God for my survival.

CHAPTER 2

ANOTHER MONDAY MORNING rolled around like clockwork and once again I found myself at work. I wasn't complaining too much about it though. I'd spent all day Sunday at home, chilling out. I'd been through a lot. The pregnancy scare had been a lot to process by itself, but stopping a robbery on top of that had really taken a lot out of me. I ended up telling some of my friends and my mother about what happened. Everybody was scared for me but glad that I'd made it through safely. My mother was terrified and I had to reassure her a bunch of times that I was well trained and careful. She made it clear to me that a bullet didn't have a name on it and that I'd be better off in life if I remembered that.

I was walking down the long hallway that led to the Briefing Room, greeting people as I normal. There was something different about that morning. I was getting glances from the in house personnel and fellow officers that I'd never met before were saying good morning and good job. I didn't know what was happening until I turned and entered the Briefing Room.

The image of every single officer in the Briefing Room standing up and applauding me as I walked in was enough to bring tears to my eyes, even though I didn't let them fall. People were smiling and nodding their heads in approval. A couple of people came up to me to shake my hand, offering "thank you's" or other congratulations. It all went on for less than a minute but it felt like forever. I smiled, nodded, and raised my hand to thank everyone.

I was relieved that no one asked me to make a speech. I didn't think that anyone would have heard about what happened but I figured that police spoke to one another and word just traveled naturally. No one had gotten shot or anything like that so it hadn't been interesting enough for the news to pick it up. I'd been thankful for that. I didn't think that I'd be able to deal with all the added pressure that the media would have out on the situation.

The sergeant cleared his throat and held his hands up, signaling the time for fanfare was over. People began to take their seats and I took one close to the back of the room. Having all of that extra attention on me definitely wasn't ideal for me but I was glad that it was over.

"Before we begin, I wanted to take a moment to acknowledge Officer Mathis and her bravery. She is new to the force and a new face to our precinct but she has a bright future ahead of her. For those of you unaware, Officer Mathis was off duty and single handedly took down an armed robber," said the sergeant. His eyes now shifted directly to mine. "Officer Mathis, your bravery, good training, and quick thinking saved a lot of lives. That situation could have gone a lot of different ways but no one was hurt, and for that, I commend you."

Another brief round of applause broke out. I smiled again. The sergeant continued on with the briefing as normal, going over the numbers and assignments for the day. I was happy for that. I didn't want to be the center of attention the entire time.

Sitting in my chair in the briefing room, I had a clear view of most of my fellow officers. I surveyed the room and despite the applause that I'd just gotten, I felt a little out of place. I felt like a traitor. They were applauding me for being a hero but I wondered how many of them would have done the same if they knew that I was sleeping with the enemy and had only days earlier had a pregnancy scare because of him.

I knew that I needed to push those thoughts out of my head but it was hard to do. I felt like I was betraying the people that I was working with. I'd been back and forth about it too much in my head. I pushed those thoughts out of my head and focused on the briefing.

When it was over I stood up and was about to head out of the room to find Brantwell who hadn't been in the briefing. I was just about to leave the room when another officer came up to me.

"The Sarge wants to see you in his office," he said.

I was little confused. I'd never been called

into anyone's office for anything. I hoped that I wasn't in trouble. "Did he say why? I asked.

"No," said the officer with a shake of his head. "He said to grab you before you went too far."

"Oh ok," I said. I thanked him for coming to tell me the message and I headed to down the hall towards his office. I didn't even realize that he'd walked passed me. When I got to his small office, he was seated behind his desk, sipping coffee and looking quite comfortable.

Sergeant Thompson was in his early 40's. He was black and mostly in shape. I hadn't had too many chances to speak with him but from what I heard, he was a nice guy. He looked up at me when I walked into the room. He motioned for me to have a seat at the chair in front of him.

"How are you doing, Mathis?" Sergeant Thompson asked.

"Good," I said. It was all I could muster since I didn't know why I was there. It didn't seem like I was in trouble since he didn't seem to be mad or anything.

"I meant every word of what I said out there during the briefing," he said. "You showed some real bravery and skill."

"Thank you, sir," I said. I didn't know if it was bravery and skill so much as me just trying to make sure no one got hurt but I'd take it.

"I think you have the potential to have a bright career on the force, if you want it that is," Thompson said. I don't know what he was expecting but I didn't have anything to say so I just stayed quiet. "I've got my eye on you. I think you can do good things, which is why I'm changing some things up."

"What do you mean?" I asked. I was a little confused.

"Officer Brantwell won't be your FTO anymore," Thompson announced. I almost smirked a little bit but stopped myself. Brantwell was my Field Training Officer or FTO for short. FTOs were older, more senior officers who got partnered up with rookies like myself to help train them on the job. Officer Brantwell and I had been paired up since the beginning. I liked him as a person but I hadn't seen any action while being under his wing. I guess stopping that robbery was really working out in my favor.

"You're going out on a new beat today with your new FTO, Officer Briggs," said Thompson.

"Damn, just like that, huh?" I asked.

"No time like the present," he replied with a smirk.

Almost on cue came a knock at the door. Thompson waved his hand letting the visitor know it was alright to come in and then stood up and motioned for me to do the same. I extended my hand and gripped his.

"I'm Taela," I said. "Nice to meet you." I nodded my head at him.

"Nice to meet you. I'm Officer Jason Briggs and I believe I'm your new FTO," he said. Officer Briggs was nothing at all like Brantwell. Where Brantwell had been old school like one of those cops you'd see on TV or something, Briggs didn't seem to be anything at all like that.

For starters, he was younger than Brantwell by a lot. By my guess, he had to be 30 at the oldest. He was white and had brunette hair that was parted off to the side in a way that made him look cooler. He had these big puppy dog brown eyes and a nice mustache. He was about 5'10" and he had a stocky build, like a fat kid who started building muscle and got in shape.

"Mathis, Brantwell has had nothing but good things to say about you so I know you two are gonna do good together," the sergeant said "Now that you've proven yourself, I think that Officer Briggs here may be a better fit for you. No offense to Brantwell but I think you're ready for a little more action and you weren't gonna get that with him."

I'd been trying not to but I smiled a little bit. I hoped that what he was saying would turn out to be true. I did want to get out there and see some more action so if this Briggs guy was going to be the person to get me out there more, I was down.

"I think you two are going to be a great fit," Sergeant Thompson said. "Now, get out there and do your jobs. I'll definitely be checking up on you two. He sounded like a coach giving a speech to his team before the big game or something like that. It was a little cheesy but I appreciated the energy.

"Let's go get our car," Briggs suggested as we stepped out of the office. We made some small talk as we headed down to the garage to get our patrol vehicle, chatting about nothing in particular. I guess we both figured there'd be time to get to know one another while we were on the road. We went through our usual inspections, making sure that the tires, gas, and all the other fluids were in good condition. We couldn't afford any mistakes or accidents while we drove.

"Mind if I drive?" Briggs asked. He was the one who had the keys so it wasn't like I could have objected anyway.

"Not at all," I said as I walked around to the passenger side. Once we were both inside we went over our route for the day and then headed out. We were quiet at first but once we stopped at our first stop light, Briggs started to talk.

"So, what made you wanna become a cop?" he asked. He turned his head to me with those big, brown eyes.

"Well, I'd been thinking about it for a while and I—" I stopped talking because I realized that Briggs was smiling and it looked like he was trying to hold back laughter or something.

"What?" I asked. I was a little annoyed. No one wanted to be laughed at.

"I'm sorry. It's just that I do this to all the rookies I get and not once has anyone of you surprised me," he said.

"What do you mean?" I asked. I didn't like to be the butt of anyone's jokes.

"I always start off by asking why you wanted

to become a cop and everyone just launches into this story and shit like it's an interview or something," he said. "It's alright to relax a little bit."

I still didn't get what was so damn funny but I just went along with it. I might not have been laughing with him but I liked that Briggs had a sense of humor. "Hmm, and what do you say when people ask you?"

He cleared his throat. "I became a cop because I have always wanted to protect and serve the people. I think that the work we do is important. I know we get a bad rap but it comes with the job," he said. I had to admit that it rolled off of his tongue perfectly.

"Is that true?" I asked.

He shook his head as he kept on driving. "Hell no," he said. "Ask most cops why they became cops and the answers are bullshit. Except for the legacies."

"Legacies?" I questioned.

"Yeah, you know them. 'My dad was a cop and so are his brothers and so was their father' and blah, blah, blah, all the way back to who knows when...don't get me wrong, I'm not knocking them. I meant every word of what I said. I'm sure Brantwell told you to wear that badge with honor because it means something and he was right about that." Briggs eyed me seriously. I knew that he wanted me to understand what he was saying. Those puppy dog eyes had a certain fire in them now because he was speaking with passion.

"I do," I said. I wanted to reassure him

"That's good," Briggs said. "So, let me tell you a little about me. I can joke around a lot but I can be a hard ass. I don't want you to forget it. Being with me means that you're ready to deal with some real stuff and not just sitting around with Brantwell, no offense to him. Now, my style of teaching is a little different from everyone else's."

"How so?" I asked. I wondered what Sergeant Thompson had been talking about when he said that Briggs was different. I guess I was about to find out.

"No shady shit or anything like that," Briggs clarified. "I'm young which means that I'm still not too far out of the academy myself. I remember what it was like and I remember being with my FTO and not taking it seriously because I felt like it was all bullshit and it was."

I just screwed my face up in confusion. Briggs was something else but I liked him.

"I want you to leave me knowing real stuff about how to navigate these streets. Are you from New York?" He asked.

"Harlem, born and raised," I said proudly. I never wanted to forget where I came from, especially not when I had the uniform on.

"That's good but understand that shit is gonna be different now that you have that uniform on," he said. "Like I said, people take us as a threat. People hate us just because we do this job and we have to be able to clench our teeth, bare it, and still protect them" he explained.

I was already seeing that Briggs and Brantwell were like night and day. Brantwell was like a parent who wanted to keep me away from everything fun but Briggs was that one cool friend that just wanted to go out and live life. I was getting more and more excited about working with Briggs. I was glad that he was being honest with me about what it meant to be an officer. I needed someone to keep it straight with me. I hoped that his talk matched up with his actions.

"But enough with the negative. The job is the job, good and bad," he said. "Outside of this, I'm originally from the Bronx but I live out in Yonkers now with my wife and our kids."

"How many do you have?" I asked.

Brantwell swelled with pride as he spoke about his kids. "I have a little boy who's two and my wife is pregnant with a little girl. We've been together five years now."

"That's amazing. I'd love to have that one day. How old are you if you don't mind me asking?" It sounded like Brantwell had his life squared away with a wife and kids at home. It was definitely a life that I hoped to live one day whenever I was ready for it.

"30," he said. "I'll be 31 in a couple of months."

"Wow, you're young," I said. "I just realized that I never asked you what really made you want to join the force."

"Well, it was my family but not the same way as everyone else. I came from a really messed up family. My father was abusive to everyone but mostly my mother. She went to the cops a couple of times about him but they just didn't seem to care. She got away eventually but she could have been out years earlier if someone had just listened to her. I became a cop because I wanted to be one of the good ones," he said. It rolled off of his tongue the same way that the other statement had, but this one sounded more genuine.

"How is your mother doing now?" I asked.

"She's good. She lives out in Queens near my brother. She has a boyfriend and he makes her happy. Last I heard my father was in Long Island somewhere," he said. He didn't sound bitter about it. He turned his head to me. "What about you?"

"Well, I told you where I'm from. My mother raised me by herself so it was just the two of us growing up. We're really close and she put pressure on me to start to figure out what I wanted to do. I looked at a bunch of things but I finally settled on being a cop. No one thought I was serious and they *damn* sure didn't think that I'd make it into the academy, let alone graduate. But I did, and here I am," I explained.

Briggs nodded his head. "That's good," he said. "I can see you going places if you want to."

"Thanks," I said. I'd been thinking about

asking him a question for a couple of minutes and I finally decided to. "What were your first couple of months on the force like?" I asked. I really wanted to know. I knew that everyone's experiences were uniquely their own but I just wanted to hear about his.

"Rough," he said with a slight smile. "That's the best way to put it. You got it good right now working the way you do but wait until you have to do mandatory OT and you are literally off of work for only enough time to go home, sleep, and then get right back out there. Not to mention the fear."

"What fear?" I asked.

"It's scary to be in the real world doing this and anyone that says they weren't scared on their first few patrols is a liar. The first time I pointed my gun at someone was when I was with Brantwell. It started off like a routine traffic stop but the guys had been carrying a lot of drugs on them. We ordered them both out of the vehicle and everything was going fine until one of them tried to sneak Brantwell. I had to pull my gun on someone for the first time and the craziest thing was that I was the one who was afraid," he said.

I was listening to every word that he said as he spoke. I knew the feeling that he was talking about because I'd felt it too when I'd stopped that robbery. It was strange to feel so powerful but still feel afraid. "I know what you mean," I said.

"I bet you do," he went on. "I had my gun on this guy and I'm just there thinking that if I made a mistake, somebody could die."

The more we talked, the more I knew that Briggs and I were going to make a good team. He had experience and wasn't afraid of telling me about it. Brantwell always wanted to talk about how to do things but Briggs just wanted me to be hands on which was what I wanted to. I knew that I was going to learn a lot from him. I was definitely excited to have gotten reassigned.

CHAPTER 3

MONDAY WAS an exciting day with my reassignment and hitting the streets with Briggs. It had definitely been a good day but I was glad to be getting off. When I got back to the locker room I checked the phone that I used to contact Young. I realized that it had been a full day since the last time we'd spoken. I hadn't heard from him since I left his house. I didn't even tell him about the robbery.

When I checked the phone I saw that he'd called me twice during the day. I didn't have a chance to call him back anyway, not with everything that was going on. I changed and left the precinct. Once I got a couple of blocks away I dialed Young.

"Wassup T?" he answered the phone.

"Hey, what are you doing right now?" I asked as I kept walking.

"Chillin, why?" he asked.

"I want you to come to the city and meet me at a hotel," I said in an excited voice.

"Everything good?" he asked with concern in his voice.

"Yeah, everything's fine. I just wanna see you," I admitted. I was smiling too.

"Aight, let me finish a couple of things and I'll come through. Just let me know when and where," he said.

"Alright, let me find a spot," I said.

I pulled out my phone and did a quick Google search for a boutique hotel further downtown. There was no way in hell I was looking for anything in the same neighborhood as the station. I found an inexpensive but nice one and took a cab downtown to it. Once I booked the room, I grabbed the key and headed upstairs.

I threw my stuff down on the bed and pulled out my phone to text Young. I gave him the address and room number and he said that he'd be one his way in a few minutes. I thought about taking a shower but I decided to wait until he got there.

A couple of minutes later there was a knock at the door and I got excited as I walked over to it. I opened the door without looking through the peephole. Young was standing there looking sexy as hell. He was wearing a gray button down shirt and a pair of dark blue jeans. His sneakers were on point of course.

He smiled as he walked in and I stepped back. He closed the door behind him and I took a step towards him. He grabbed me up in his arms like I weighed nothing. We kissed passionately for a full minute before we stopped. Both of us were smiling goofily at the other.

"Mmm," he growled at me, "I missed you." He was holding me tight just the way I liked.

"I missed you too," I said as I patted his arm for him to let me down. "I got an idea."

"What?" He asked.

"I was gonna take a shower before you got here, but I decided to wait for you," I said.

His smirk turned into a full blown grin after that. He didn't even say anything. He just started taking his clothes off. I started to laugh but I did the same. I went into the bathroom and turned the shower on, making sure not to put it at my normal hot temperature.

Young walked into the bathroom a minute later. His dick was semi hard. His body was a work of art with all the colorful tattoos he had. I went into the shower and let the warm water hit my body. Young was standing there staring at me so I decided to put on a little show.

With the water running all down my body, I started to lather myself up with the soap. I was rubbing it all over my titties and with my other hand I was playing with my pussy. Young was getting turned on. His dick was getting harder and harder by the second. Seeing him get so turned on was having the same effect on me.

Young walked towards me and stepped into the shower alongside me. I was grateful that I'd opted for one of the nicer rooms because the bathroom was bigger than other rooms and the shower was a nice size.

The water hit the two of us and we started kissing again. Young started to grip all over my body with his strong, firm hands. He played with my ass and put his fingers in my pussy and played around. Our foreplay was more intense than normal because of the water and the steam coming from the shower.

I reached out of the shower onto the top of the sink for the condom that I'd grabbed earlier and brought to the bathroom. After that pregnancy scare, there was no way that I was about to try and have sex with him again without using a condom. I handed it to Young who slipped it on his dick.

I was facing Young from the front. He once again picked me up like I was nothing but this time he positioned my body so that I could slip onto his dick. It slid in like it was made for it. I wrapped my arms around his neck and we kept on kissing. He pressed my back against the wall of the bathroom and started to dig me out

It was pretty foggy in the bathroom but I could make out our shapes in the foggy bathroom mirror. I felt every thrust of Young's hips as he worked his body in and out of mine.

"Fuck me baby," I moaned.

"You like this shit, Tae?" Young asked. He stopped kissing me and looked me deep into my eyes. He sped himself up a little bit.

"Yes, Young," I moaned. I knew that I had to be making faces and stuff but it felt so damn good to me. Young was blessed to have a big stick and was skilled in how to use it. I was on the verge of coming.

"Tell me you like this shit," he commanded as he sped himself up even more and then moved his hips in a more circular motion.

"Oh shit!" I said as I felt my body shake with an intense orgasm. I couldn't even say anything to him. He must have been as turned on by me because he came soon after.

After we finished, we took a real shower together and then got out of the bathroom. We thought about going out to eat but decided on just ordering room service since the hotel had a nice menu. I got some salmon and mashed potatoes and he ordered a steak.

We were talking like normal and stuff but there was something in my mind that he didn't know about. I wanted to tell him about the robbery and all that stuff but I just couldn't. As much as I felt the urge to, I just didn't know how he'd take it. Regardless of how much we pretended otherwise, we were still on opposites sides of the law and he might not have seen things how I did when it came to the thief and stuff so I just decided not to bring it up.

"Tell me about your family," Young said.

"Not much to tell," I said. "It's just me and my mother. It's always just been the two of us. My father wasn't around growing up. You know how that goes."

Young nodded his head.

"She and I are close. Growing up, I didn't really want for much. We weren't rich but we weren't poor either," I explained. "What about you?"

"It was me, my mom's, and my little brother and sister growing up. I was pretty much the man of the house. My mother didn't like it when I hit the streets and started hustling but once she figured out that she couldn't talk me out of it, she just stopped bringing it up," he said.

"Where are they now?" I asked.

"My brother is in college and my sister is in high school," he said. "I ended up paying whatever was left over after his financial aid and scholarships." I could tell that he was proud of him.

"You ever thought about going back to school?" I asked him.

"Nah," he said. "I see the value in college

but I know it's not for me. You can only be who you are and this is who I am. But me being me doesn't have to stop them from doing them. I keep my world apart from theirs and all that."

I nodded my head and opened my mouth to speak but Young held a finger up to stop me. I was about to ask him what he was doing but he held his finger to his lips for me to be quiet.

"Yo, I really wanna say something to you but I don't want you to interrupt," he said.

I nodded my head. I wondered what was on his mind.

"I'm really feeling you, Tae. Seriously," he said as he looked me in the eyes. "I don't let nobody get close to me, especially not women. I don't like distractions. But you're different. We talk and I end up telling you stuff that I've never told anyone else. There's something special about you that's got me falling so fast. And I know that this is sudden and shit like that but I just don't see no point in waiting. I want you to be my girl...officially."

"Yes," I said without hesitation. I leaned forward and kissed him. I wondered how long he'd been thinking about it. It felt good to know that Young felt so comfortable around me. He could be this big thug and all of these other things outside but when he was with me, we were just cool. I didn't have to think about becoming his girl because I felt the same way as him.

We were both so excited about taking the next step in our relationship. It had been a while since I'd been in a relationship but it felt good to be doing it again with Young. There was something different about him that just made me know that we'd work out.

That night we made love for the first time. I say for the first time because that time was different from the others. We took out time, slowly kissing one another with more passion than ever before. Young rubbed my entire body down and as we made love, our fingers interlocked with each other's.

I went to bed that night satisfied and hoping that no one noticed I was wearing the same clothes two days in a row.

CHAPTER 4

IT HAD BEEN three wonderful weeks as boyfriend and girlfriend for Young and I. We'd been really getting to know one another better and were taking things slow. The only problem that we were having was that we were getting tired of all the sneaking around. We wanted to be able to just go out on a date like normal people but we couldn't. Us going back and forth from each of our apartments was becoming boring. Not to mention that the hotel room thing had lost everything that made it sexy in the first place.

"We gotta switch up," Young said one day out of the blue. We were at his house watching some show on Netflix.

"What you talkin 'bout?" I asked. My head was on his lap and he was playing in my hair.

"We should get outta here" he said in a way that let me know he wasn't just talking about the apartment. "Let's go away for the weekend? Nothing crazy. Just something that's not New York. Feel me?"

I sat up and looked at him. "That would be nice, like really nice. I can't afford it right now though. I've only gotten two checks so I haven't been able to put much away," I said.

Young screwed his face up at me. "You think I'm gonna let you come out ya pocket? This is on me. We just gotta come up with a destination."

I smiled at Young and kissed him on the cheek. I felt a little bad when I thought about the source of his money but I pushed those thoughts out of my mind in favor of thinking about spending real time with my man.

"Which weekend?" I asked him.

"How about this upcoming one?" he responded with a serious look on his face.

"What? Are you crazy? It's already Wednesday," I said. "That's no time to plan."

"What's there to plan?" He asked. "It's only

a weekend. How about L.A.? You ever been there?"

"No I haven't," I said. "I've definitely always wanted to go but I think for a weekend trip we should do something on the East Coast since we won't have to travel for as long. How about Miami?" I'd only been to Miami once when I first turned 21. I'd loved it and had wanted to go back but couldn't find the time.

"Miami sounds nice," he said. "Mmm, you in a bathing suit. Drinks in our hands. And we can walk down the boardwalk, hand in hand like normal people."

"Mmm, that sounds good. I get to be all hugged up on my man for real," I said. "Do you need my help with anything? I can help you book places for cheap."

"Nah," he said, "I got this. I'll book it all. I'll let you know what info I need from you."

"I'm so excited!" I said. "This is gonna be fun. It's so spur of the moment but I'm with it."

"I'm glad you were down," Young said. "You match my speed."

"No, you match *my* speed," I joked with him.

The next two days seemed to breeze by and

I couldn't have been happier about that either. I was definitely ready to be on my way out of New York and on my way to Miami with my man where we could finally get a taste of what it felt like to be a *real* couple: holding hands, going on dates, all of that.

Young handled all of the reservations and booking the flights. He'd been smart about it too. Neither him or myself were on the same flight going or coming. We arrived in Miami at separate times with him getting there first. Our flights didn't leave from the same terminal or airline at the airport either. We thought it would be better to be safe than sorry in the long run.

The entire time that we were on our way down there, we kept in touch via text. I kept gushing over how excited I was to be going away with him. When he got to the hotel and sent me a picture from the balcony of our room that overlooked the beach and the water, I was so happy. It felt like a dream come true.

When I got off my flight I headed to grab my bags and then I took a cab to the hotel. Young had sent me the address and room number before I got there so when I got to the hotel I headed straight up to the room. I knocked on the door and Young answered it. I was definitely ready to get inside and get out of my flight clothes. Miami was hot as hell.

When Young opened the door, I knew that we'd made the right decision. Miami was doing my baby right. He opened the door looking like a snack.

He must've really been feeling the tropical weather because he had on a red and white speckled Hawaiian shirt and a hair of khaki shorts that hugged his muscular legs. On his feet, he'd traded his pair of sneakers for a nice pair of boat shoes that went with the shirt. I could smell his cologne coming off of him.

"Damn baby, you look good," I said to him as I walked in. He grabbed me up in his arms and kissed me passionately. Usually this would have kept going for a little while but he broke it up early.

"We got time for that later," he said. "I got some plans for us. Go freshen up."

"Plans?" I asked as I carried my bag over to the bed. "Like what? I was thinking we could just chill out for a little bit."

"It's a surprise," Young said excitedly. "I

gotta treat you how I wish I could treat you in New York."

"You treat me fine, no matter where we are" I said truthfully.

"You know what I mean," he said. He was excited like a little kid. "Just hurry up."

"Alright, let me go into the bathroom," I said.

I got ready in half an hour or so. I jumped into the shower and when I got out I picked out a nice dress to wear. It was casual but still could pass as dressy. I didn't know where we were headed so I wanted to be prepared for anything.

Young and I left the hotel together and for the first time ever, we walked hand in hand down the street as a couple. I knew we must've looked good because people kept taking glances at us like we were celebrities or something. Our skin looked amazing in the Miami sun and the breeze didn't stop blowing gently. It felt like paradise.

The two of us walked for a couple of minutes down Collins Avenue before heading over to the beachside. We took our time as we went. The air was warm but there was slight breeze blowing that felt great against my skin. Young and I walked and talked as we went. I think that more than anything, we were happy to just be able to be around one another and just hang out. We ended up at a seafood restaurant that Young wanted to check out. He said that he'd heard good things about it from a friend of his who was a Miami native.

We got inside and Young ordered us a bottle of wine. The waiter was nice and explained the whole menu to us. I ended up getting the crab cakes and Young got the surf and turf. I should've known that he'd order steak.

"This food is delicious," I said as I ate. When I say that everything was on point, I meant it. The service in the place was five stars. The decor was amazing. It was tropical and upscale but didn't feel stuffy or old. The food was the best part though. My steak cut like butter and the lobster and mashed potatoes were seasoned perfectly and melted in my mouth. I tasted Young's crab cake and I swore that the crab's must've just been caught.

"Nah, it's better than delicious," he said as he dipped his lobster in the butter. "Are you having a good time?"

"Yeah," I nodded. "Of course. Are you?"

"Yeah. We only getting started," Young smiled.

When we left the restaurant, we strolled the boardwalk and then decided to walk along the beach close to the water. The sun was almost completely set but there was still a little glow over the horizon. The mix of the yellow and orange with the water looked like a painting.

"I don't want you paying for me everywhere we go," I said to Young. We'd been quiet as we were walking. I knew that Young wanted to take care of me and all of that but I was also fine with being able to take care of myself.

"Why not?" He asked. "I got it. You just said the other day that you ain't have enough time to start saving from work."

"I know that, but I'm not broke either," I said it a little more rudely than I'd meant to. My mother raised me to be independent so it was weird to have him trying to pay for everything for me.

"Chill, chill," he said. He dropped my hand and playfully held up his in retreat. "I know what you mean. But I just wanna take care of you. How about I just take care of this trip and we see how it goes in the future? Deal?" He held out his hand for me to shake.

"Deal. I'm gonna find a way to pay you back though" I said as I shook his hand. "So, what's something I don't you about you yet?" I wanted to change the topic to something lighter.

"Hmmm," he thought out loud. "I was a Boy Scout when I was growing up."

I burst out laughing at that. "What? You? I can't imagine it."

"Damn, why couldn't I have been a Boy Scout?" he asked in a playful hurt way.

"It's not that you couldn't. It just that I wouldn't have imagined it," I said. Imagining Young as a Boy Scout was funny enough. "How was it?'

"It was cool. It taught me how to work as a part of a team," he said. "What's something I don't know about you?"

I got really playful for a minute. Young was walking closer to the water than I was. "You don't know that I used to run track!" I yelled as I pushed him as hard as I could towards the water. He was way bigger than me so all I really did was knock him off balance but it gave me just enough of a chance to start running. I wasn't lying either. I took off like a bat out of hell, holding onto my shoes in one hand and my the bottom of my dress in the other. I was laughing the whole way.

I turned around, expecting Young to be far behind me but he was right on my tail and it looked like he was jogging. He sped up a little bit and grabbed me, scooping me up in his arms and spinning me around.

"You wanna play around, right?" he asked as he laughed. He was walking towards the water.

"What you doing? Young, don't drop me in the water!" I went from laughing and joking to dead serious. I wasn't playing with him either. I wasn't about to get my damn hair wet, and definitely not my outfit.

"Oh, now you don't wanna play around?" Young chuckled as he playfully lowered me. He dipped me low toward the water and I yelled out loud.

"I'm sorry!" I screamed.

"What?" he asked in a loud voice.

"I'm sorry!" I said again. He walked back to the beach and put me back on the ground. I fixed my clothes. "Damn, why you play so much?"

"Me?" he asked. "You started it. Don't start nothing you can't finish."

"Hmph," I said with a fake attitude. He didn't know what he was getting started.

We were only about five minutes away from the hotel but I didn't speak to him for those last few blocks. I was definitely trying to play up the hurt girlfriend routine, especially since I wouldn't have a chance to do it once we were back in New York. I wanted him to think that I was mad with him. When we got back in the room he went to the bathroom and then went out on the balcony to smoke weed.

I wanted Young to think that I was mad with him because I really wanted to thank him for the trip and I had some really raunchy shit in mind. I went to the bathroom and changed out of my dress and slipped into this new lingerie that I'd bought just for the trip. It was red and lacy and hugged each of my curves. I tied my hair up in a messy bun and applied a fresh coat of lip gloss.

Young was still outside on the balcony so he didn't hear me come out. His back was to me and he was leaning over the railing, smoke blowing from his mouth. The sun had gone all the way down but the light of boardwalk still gave off a little light. It was dimly lit at best which meant that people could probably still see us. I didn't mind though.

I stepped out onto the balcony barefoot. There was a warm breeze coming over the water that kissed my skin. I tapped Young on the back and he turned around. His eyes almost bugged out of his head when he looked at me.

"What's goin—" He tried to ask what was happening but I held up a finger to stop him. I was in control and I was keeping it.

"Shh," I said. "I told you I wanted to thank you. Just smoke."

I wrapped one hand around his neck and with the other I undid the buckle on his shorts. I unzipped them and put my hand inside of his boxer briefs. I grabbed at his dick and played with it until it got semi hard. Using both of my hands, I pulled the front of the shorts down so his dick could be free.

"What you doin?" Young asked, half surprised and half turned on.

I didn't say anything to him. I just dropped

down to my knees and took his dick in my mouth. I bobbed up and down on it until it was rock hard and then I got really nasty, using my hand and stuff. I knew Young had to be in heaven between the head and the weed. I was making all kinds of noises and he started to moan to.

"Damn Tae," he moaned out loud. I was glad that we were outside and didn't have to keep quiet.

My hands jerked him up and down ad my mouth kept it wet. I was good at giving head and Young putting his hand on the back of my head to push it further down on his dick let me know that I was doing a good job.

I just knew that Young had to be on the verge of coming and I didn't want him to do that so I stopped. I reached into my bra and handed him the condom.

Young started kissing me passionately. His head moved down to my neck and I hopped into his arms.

"You want this dick ma?" he whispered in my ear with his deep voice.

"Yes, baby," I cooed back. He slipped the condom on his dick and lowered me down to the floor. He took two steps towards the sliding door that led back inside and only stopped walking when he saw that I wasn't moving.

"What happened?" he asked. He sounded a little disappointed. He must've thought he wasn't gonna get any.

"Why you going inside?" I asked him. The look on my face let him know what I meant. He smirked.

"You serious? Somebody could see," he said as he started looking around like he was expecting someone to fly up to the 12th floor to see us.

"The closest hotel with a balcony facing this way three blocks that way in the dark. The people on the beach would have to be looking for us," I said. Something about being in Miami was making me feel more adventurous. We hadn't even spent a full night yet and we were already having the time of our lives.

To prove my point, I reached behind me and unstrapped my bra, letting my breasts free. My panties hit the floor right afterwards and I turned around giving him a nice view of my ass. I knew he wasn't about to turn it down. I bent myself over the railing and gasped when Young pushed himself inside of me. He didn't take it slow this time. He was rougher than usual I actually liked it.

Young wrapped his hand around my neck and pulled me back so he could hit it better. I don't think I'd ever been hornier in my life. My pussy was dripping with my own juices and Young was only making more come out of me. It was like we moved like one person.

After a couple of minutes he made it clear that he was about to come. "Fuck! Damn Tae! This shit is good!" he grunted as he pounded away.

"Mmm," I moaned.

"Fuck!" He moaned as his body shook and he jerked forward. I felt his knees get weak for a second or two before he stood up and pulled himself out of me. That nut must have taken a lot out of him because he was breathing hard.

"Damn Tae," he said. "I don't know what got into you but I liked it."

"Me too," I said with a little laugh.

We cleaned up and then got in the bed with each other to just chill out. Young ordered a bottle of champagne that we still hadn't opened. I was resting my head on his chest as we watched some movie on HBO. Everything was going great with our night until Young's phone rang. I knew from being around him that he was one of those people who gave different contacts different ringtones. I'd never heard the ringer that called him late that night but when he heard it he jumped out of bed to answer it.

"Yo?" He answered the phone. "I told you not to hit my line unless..." His voice trailed off.

I was only half paying attention to him on the phone. I wouldn't have noticed anything but he started getting louder. I didn't know who he was on the phone with but something wasn't going the way it was supposed to, or at least that's what I pieced together.

"I don't understand how nobody knows what the fuck is going on," Young said as he paced back and forth. He'd taken a quick shower and had put on a pair of black boxer briefs. He seemed to be annoyed and worried but still hadn't said anything to me. I knew it probably wasn't the moment but I was getting turned on watching him look like such a boss.

"I'm out of town but I'm on my way back to take care of my business," Young said. I'd given up on pretending not to be listening. Whatever he was dealing with was probably illegal and I shouldn't have been listening but I couldn't help it. He wasn't telling me anything.

"Nah, I'm on the next thing smokin' back to New York. Word," he said before he hung up the phone and put it on the charger.

It was like Young had forgotten that I was there. He was mumbling curse words to himself and throwing his stuff into the duffle bag that he'd brought with him. It wasn't until he started to put on his pants that I finally spoke.

"Young," I called out to him but he didn't respond. He put his sneakers on and reached out for his shirt. "Young!" I called louder.

"What?" he answered as he finished getting his clothes on. He grabbed his bag. "Look, I got an emergency situation back in the city and I gotta get back. I might go MIA for a minute but don't bug out, ok? I'll hit you up when I can," he said. He turned to leave and headed for the door. "Charge whatever you want to the room. It's paid for till Sunday and my card is good."

Young walked out of the room and the door clicked behind him.

CHAPTER 5

I CALLED Young a bunch of times that night but didn't get any answer. I sent him text messages and all that. I got no response back. I was worried about him. He'd left so abruptly that I didn't even really have a chance to say bye or anything.

I ended up checking out of the hotel that next morning. I wasn't about to stay in Miami alone, paid for room or not. It just wasn't the same without Young being there. The entire point of us going to Miami was to be together.

When I got back to New York that Saturday, I hit Young up again. When I didn't get an answer, I decided to just play the waiting game.

Friday rolled around and that meant that it

had been almost a week since I'd last heard from Young. I was definitely concerned about him. He could have been hurt or dead somewhere and I wouldn't have known it I thought for a moment that him or his crew might have gotten locked up but everything had been quiet at the briefings. In fact, there hadn't been a word about him or his crew the entire week. It wasn't strange but it did make me wonder where he'd gone or if he was even still in New York. I didn't know where his "business" took him.

I'd been wracking my nerves trying to figure it out. I knew that he told me that I shouldn't worry but what the fuck did he expect me to do? He literally got up in the middle of the night and hopped on a flight back to New York with no explanation. When he did that, I felt hurt and disrespected. I was risking so much just to see him and be with him and he hadn't valued it.

I was at work that morning with Young on my mind. I just wished that there was someone I could talk to. I couldn't really go to my friends with it because I couldn't be honest with them. I'd already gotten judgement just by having a dance with him so if I said that I was dating him, it definitely wouldn't have been good.

And there was no way in hell that I was going to go to my mother about it either. I loved her dearly but she definitely knew how to drive a point when she felt she was right. She'd given me shit for leaving Reggie alone. Even though I explained to her why I just didn't see it for him, she kept right on going.

Oh shit, I thought. There actually was someone that I could talk to, and that person might have some answers for me. I'd completely forgotten that I'd seen that picture of Young and officer Harris together. I didn't know how close they were or how often they spoke but I thought I should at least reach out to him and let him know that I'm aware of him.

The briefing was about to start in a couple of minutes. I spotted Harris at the back of the room, sipping a cup of coffee and leaning against the wall. I grabbed a cup for myself and went and stood next to him. I held the cup over my mouth as I spoke and mumbled, "Any news for me?" loud enough for him and only him to hear.

"I was wondering if you were ever gonna

say something. He said you were smart. Let's talk after work. Meet me at Shifty's," Harris said.

I didn't say anything. I just nodded my head and walked away to grab a seat before the briefing. Harris and I didn't normally speak to one another and I didn't want to look suspicious.

After the briefing, Briggs and I headed out on patrol. It was a beautiful Friday morning. It was warm but not too hot. I was glad for it too.

"Why do people always do that?" I asked as I nodded my head towards us. The timer on the crosswalk had already been down to three seconds when this woman darted out into the street with her stroller.

"I don't know," Briggs said as we pulled off. The woman was still in the street trying to get across. "People think that having strollers gives them the right to go wherever."

The two of us drove along, keeping our eyes out for anything strange and waiting for something to come through on the radio. We were inside of our patrol zone and it had been mostly quiet as the morning went on.

"Car 8951 come in please, this is dispatch. We have a report of domestic violence in your vicinity. Are you free to respond? Over." The voice of the radio dispatcher came through abruptly and in a hurry. My heart started beating fast. I was still getting used to that part of the job. I never knew what call was going to come through the radio on a daily basis. It could be something simple or it could be something life and death. I was trying to get myself ready to deal with whatever happened.

We took the call and got the address of a brownstone. I was still behind the wheel so I sped up. When it came to domestic abuse calls, you never knew what you were going to get. With the siren blaring, I turned the corner and headed down the block towards the address. I was looking for the right building number but I didn't have to look for too long.

I pulled the car over in front of a woman who was crying hysterically. Instinctively I hopped out and so did Briggs. The woman practically threw herself onto the roof of our car. She was African American and looked like she was in her early to mid 30's. Her hair was all messed up and the blouse that she was wearing was torn. Her right eye was black and swelling. It looked pretty fresh.

"Oh God! Oh Lord!" she cried out in pain. Briggs headed towards her but I held up my hand to stop him from getting closer. A woman would want to hear from another woman in a moment like this.

"Ma'am, I'm Officer Mathis and this is my partner Officer Briggs. Please wait here by the car. An ambulance is a block or two away. Is the suspect armed?" I asked. I was being forceful but still gentle. There was a sense of urgency in my voice but I wasn't trying to scare her.

"No," she managed to stop crying just enough to say.

"I'll take lead," Briggs said to me and I nodded.

We stepped down two steps to get to the basement apartment of the brownstone. Briggs was walking ahead of me, being cautious with every step. I was watching his back but also trying to make sure that I paid attention to how he did everything. One day I'd be doing this with someone else and I'd be in his spot.

Before he went all the way inside the entryway that led to the main door, Briggs banged loudly on the outer door. "Sir, this is

NYPD, we are coming inside!" Briggs's authoritative voice boomed into the house.

We heard some walking and shuffling on the other side of the door and then the bottom lock unlocked, followed by the opening of the door.

The man was bald, brown skin, and average height with a stocky build. His eyes were bloodshot and low and he smelled like last call at a dive bar. He was clearly drunk but looked seemed to be sober enough.

"What?" he asked, gruffly. "What the fuck y'all want?"

"Sir, we got a report of domestic disturbance at this address. Your wife or girlfriend is outside. What's going on?" Briggs asked.

The guy stepped further into the house and we followed. It was a nicely decorated place, despite the mess.. There were pictures on the wall and it smelled like food had just finished being cooked. I realized in that instant that it was probably best not to judge books by their cover.

"What the fuck you mean what's going on?" The guy asked. He walked further into the house into the living room. A couple of things had been knocked onto the floor from what it looked like. It was obvious that there had been a scuffle.

Briggs continued taking the lead, talking to the man and trying to calm him down. He was drunk and a little belligerent but Briggs seemed to be working his charm on him. We'd still need to get the woman to press charges. I decided that Briggs had the situation under control. I signaled to him that I was going to head back outside to check on the woman.

I turned around and started walking towards the door.

"You bitches always turning your backs to me!" That was the abuser's booming voice behind me as I felt something hit me hard in the back of the head with force. I didn't fall but I did stumble towards the door. I turned around, preparing for another attack but thankfully it wasn't coming. Briggs had already moved on the guy and was wrestling him to the ground. He had a knee in his back and was grabbing at his handcuffs.

Pissed off wasn't even the word. If he wasn't already on the floor, I would've kicked his ass. Instead I helped Briggs put the cuffs on that son of a bitch. Briggs lifted him up and pushed him roughly out of the house. He stumbled into the wall.

"What the fuck?! I'm suing. This some bull-shit," the drunk guy slurred.

"Shut the fuck up!" Briggs said loudly. "You assaulted a cop and beat up your girlfriend. You're going away for a long time."

"Man, fuck that bitch," he slurred. I wondered if he was talking about me or me or the woman outside. Briggs grabbed the guy back up and walked him quickly back outside. The ambulance was parked outside and the EMT's were starting to work on the woman. She was in bad shape but she'd heal.

Briggs put the guy in the back of the car. I went ahead and got a statement from the woman and told her that we'd be following back up with her. I asked if she'd be pressing charges and she said yes. Even if she didn't, he'd be going down either way.

The EMT's took the woman to the hospital. The drunk guy had fallen asleep in the backseat. As Briggs pulled the car off I had to crack a window to let out some of the smell that was coming off the drunk guy.

"Are you alright?" Briggs asked after a

couple of minutes of silence. "I know the EMT's checked you out but I just gotta ask."

"I'm good," I said. "It looked worse than it felt. Thanks for having my back."

"Always," Briggs said in a reassuring way. "We're partners. To hell with all that FTO stuff."

"I appreciate it," I said. I meant it. That day had proven to me for sure that I needed to be on the lookout when I was on patrol but it did feel good to know that Briggs really had my back. I didn't know what I would have done without him.

CHAPTER 6

IT TOOK Briggs and I a little while to fill out all the paperwork that we needed to do for the domestic abuse call that we'd gotten earlier. The back of my head was still a little sore from where I'd gotten hit. I hated that I'd let that guy get the best of me but I had to remind myself that it was nothing more than a sucker punch.

I was stepping just a *little* bit lighter because of the soreness as I headed to the locker room after my shift ended. As I started to change into my street clothes I decided to pop two aspirin. I might have been going to a bar but I didn't actually plan on drinking.

As I was getting dressed I was buzzing with

curiosity. I knew that going to meet Harris could be a huge disappointment but there was also a chance that it would be just what I needed. Either way, I needed to make sure that I got there and asked every question that I could. I wanted to know where he was and why I hadn't heard from him. I knew that some of the answers might not be stuff that I wanted to hear but it was a risk that I was willing to take.

I finished changing and grabbed my bag. As I headed out of the locker room I couldn't help but think that a couple of weeks ago I'd been patiently waiting, well more like begging for, some excitement. *Be careful what you wish for*, I thought to myself. I headed down the long and twisting hallways that led towards the entrance that the employees used.

"Damn, it's been one of those days, huh?" Officer Latimore said. She was an older officer who stayed around the station and worked the security door in the back. She was nice and only a couple of years away from retirement, though she'd tell you that she could still kick some ass if she wanted.

"What you mean?" I asked. I stopped walking and too my headphone out.

"Unless you living inside a mirror, your shirt is on inside out...and backwards too if I'm not mistaken," she said with a chuckle.

I looked down at the t-shirt I was wearing and sure enough it was on the wrong way just like she'd said. How the hell could I have gotten that wrong? "I have a lot on my mind," I said. "Today was something else." *And it's still not over*, I thought to myself.

I thanked Latimore for pointing out my big ass mistake before I hit the streets. I headed back to the locker room. I double checked myself in the mirror to make sure that everything was on the right way and in good condition this time around. I didn't want to have to come back to change again. Once I was sure, I headed back out.

As I stepped out onto the street I got a little anxious about the meeting.. It had been in the back of my mind all day that I had plans to meet up with Officer Harris after work at Shifty's. I wanted to know what, if any, info he had on Young. I put a little pep in my step.

The walk to Shifty's wasn't too bad. I got there a little while after I left the precinct.

It seemed to be a standard bar with booths

on one side, tables in the middle and a very long bar on the other side. It attracted a mixed crowd but despite the name, most people that were regulars were clean cut.

I spotted Officer Harris at a booth off to the left side in the middle. He had something brown in his glass with a cherry at the bottom. I walked over to the booth and sat down across from him. His head was down and he didn't even look up at me when I sat down.

"How'd you know it was me?" he asked me.

I thought about what he meant and realized that he was talking about his connection to Young. "He has a picture of the two of you up in his house. It looked like your graduation," I said. I wasn't about to tell him *why* I was in Young's apartment. If he wanted to take a guess then that was his business. I didn't know Officer Harris to tell him *my* business.

He finally looked up at me and took a sip of his drink. "I told that nigga to take that down," he said, half annoyed and half smirking. "We went to high school with each other. Back then *we* were young and he was just Eric."

"And you two are still close after all this

time," I said. "How'd that happen?" I would have thought that they might have naturally grown apart since they clearly went down two different paths in life.

"E wasn't just a friend, he was more like a brother to me, still is. We know each other's families. We done been through some real shit together. I've always told him that he could be whatever he wanted to be. He's smart as hell but he got addicted to the fast money and the wild life. I don't judge him though cause I know he's a good dude on the inside despite the shit he does," he explained.

I realized then how much I didn't know about Young. It was nice hear someone talk about him in such a positive way. Literally no one had anything good to say about him so it was good to hear something nice for a change. Young and Officer Harris went back a long ways but it was cool to see that they still had a bond after all this time. I hoped that meant that he'd be able to offer me some answers since the two of them were so close.

I was surprised that he hadn't asked about my relationship with Young but I decided to tell him about it because he'd opened up to me. I planned on keeping it brief though. "I've been seeing...dating Young for about two months," I said. "I think I love him."

I cared about Young a lot and I'd been going back and forth in my head for a little while about how I felt about him. I knew that my feelings for him were deep and I wanted to explore them further. It felt weird to be admitting it out loud and especially to Harris of all people but it was how I felt.

"That's definitely not what I was expecting you to say," Harris said. He raised an eyebrow and gave me a look that said he thought I was being foolish. To people looking at the situation from the outside, it probably looked like I was doing the absolute most but I wasn't in over my head, at least not yet. "You should be careful."

"What's that supposed to mean?" I asked. Harris and I were only barely familiar with one another so I don't know why he felt the need to pass along warnings.

"Man look, I'm not trying to get involved in your love affair or nothing like that," Harris said. "But I do know this much, I might not have known what route he was going to take when we were kids but I know what path he's on now and so do you."

"And what's that supposed to mean?" I was curious about why he was giving me such an ominous warning. Harris didn't know me from Eve and unless we were both on duty, I didn't need him looking out for me.

"We're cops and even though we both care about him, we both know *what* he is," Harris said as he looked me squarely in the eyes. A moment passed between us with neither of us blinking.

"And yet, that didn't stop *you* from slipping me his number," I said. He didn't say anything. He finally broke our gaze as he looked down at his drink.

"So what is it that you want to know? You clearly need something from me otherwise I wouldn't be here," he said.

"Where is he? I haven't heard from him in almost a week," I said. I was trying to hide my worry but it was obvious how much I cared. I didn't wanna sound like some kinda thirsty chick, even though I was sure that's what Harris thought I was. I didn't care what he thought of me though.

"He's fine," Harris said. "He's alive and well and right here in the city. He's laying low right now." It was like he could read my mind and knew that I'd been bugging out about where he was and what condition. "He got word about something going down, something big. A rival gang was...is...trying to take over some of his territory. You know he's the boss so he ain't gonna take that shit lying down. He's coming up with a plan to take out the whole group from top to bottom."

For all of his talk about us being cops and how I shouldn't be with Young, he damn sure knew a lot about Young's plan. I was sure he wasn't sharing any of that info with the NYPD but I was minding my business. It was clear that we were both in really deep.

"So why hasn't he hit me up?" I asked.

"No distractions, that's my only guess" he said. "Rule number one in Young's book is no distractions, and he might care about you but he's not about to let you take his eye off of what he wants. Right now that's someone's head on a platter. He's been working and making moves on the low. Even NYPD don't know about the key players he's knocked out of play."

I didn't want to hear any more. I was always curious about Young's other life but I didn't know if I needed to hear details. "Can you get a message to him for me?"

Harris shook his head. "No can do," he said.

"Why not?"

"For one, you're still in a position where you can walk away free and clear. Use that to your advantage. There's gonna be a time where you can't say that," Harris said. He seemed to have a bit of regret in his eyes. I'd imagine that keeping Young's secrets for all of these years couldn't have been easy but that was his burden to bear, not mine. "Another thing is that I try not to involve myself in his business like that. What you two have going on is between y'all, not me."

The fucking nerve of Harris to try and pull some bullshit like that on me. How can he claim that he's not gonna involve himself in Young's business when he just sat with me and told me every damn thing that he's been up to? It was stuff that I was sure I wasn't supposed to know about.

I was also getting tired of Harris' little warnings to me. Like I said, I get where he was coming from. Being friends with Young couldn't really be easy, not when you two were on different sides of the law. I know that he was probably trying to save me some from having to go through some of the same stuff that he went through but I needed to go through it myself.

Harris stood up, signaling the end of the conversation. He reached into his pocket, pulling out a $10 dollar bill and tucking it neatly under the drink. He started to head towards the door. I stood up and followed him. He was the only person that I knew that could contact Young for me and I needed to know that he'd be passing my message along.

"Tell him that he needs to call me," I said to Harris once we'd gotten outside of the bar. He stopped and looked at me. Without another word, he shook his head and walked off down the street headed in the opposite direction.

I started walking the other way and stopped to grab a cab on the corner. After less than a few minutes, a black car pulled over for me. I told the driver where I was going and asked him to turn on the radio.

Staring out the window, I couldn't help but

to cry tears of frustration. Harris' ass had better pass that message along. That wasn't even where the frustration came from though. The day had been a roller coaster of emotions and I was tired of holding them all inside. The tears streamed silently down my face as I headed home.

CHAPTER 7

When I got home a little while after meeting Harris, I hadn't stopped crying. It felt like I was letting go of all the bullshit that I'd been holding onto all week long. I guess that when it came to my feelings for Young, I'd have to deal with them alone. I didn't know who I could really talk to about then. Harris wasn't my friend so I wasn't about to start sharing secrets with him. I just hoped that he passed along my message.

Everything with Young was getting on my nerves. I was kind of frustrated with him for not hitting me up but once Harris explained what was going on, it made it a little easier to understand. I knew that Young had business to handle but I wished that he would have hit me up.

Young was very special to me and as I laid in my bed, that was all I could think about. He didn't know it but he'd had an impression on me. I knew that he cared about me and all I wanted to do was talk to him. I wanted to tell him about work and lay in the bed with him.

I reached into my bag and grabbed the disposable phone that I used to contact Young. I held it in my hand for a few minutes and thought about dialing his number. In the end I decided not to do it. I didn't want to set myself up for more failure. He had my number and could definitely reach out to me if he wanted to. I'd just wait for him to call or text me.

I ended up pretty much crying myself to sleep. While I drifted off, I let my mind think about the good times with Young. I just knew that he had to be missing me the same way that I was missing him. I thought about Miami and how what seemed like it was going to be the perfect trip ended up getting cut short.

When I finally did manage to get to sleep, I dreamt of Young, of course. In the dream, the two of us were on a beach somewhere. It wasn't Miami. It wasn't even some place that I'd been before. We were each on beach chairs next to one another. The sun felt warm on my skin and the water was so clear that I could see on forever. Young and I were holding hands and even though neither of us was speaking, I knew that we were in love.

Ring.

Ring.

Ring.

The ringing of the phone next to me sounded like it was coming from somewhere far away. Slowly the beach and the sun faded away and I woke up to the darkness of my bedroom. As I woke up, it started to register to me that it wasn't my regular phone ringing, it was the phone that I used to call Young. I sat up in bed and started feeling around for the phone. I found it down by my feet and grabbed it just as it stopped ringing.

"Shit!" I cursed out loud.

I didn't even have to look at the number. Young was the only one who had it so he had to have been the caller. I went to my call log so that I could call back but I was stopped by a sound coming from the living room. It sounded like someone had knocked at the door but my phone said it was one o'clock in the morning so I didn't know who the hell that could be.

The sound came again, harder and louder this time. I was sure that it was someone at the door but I was wondering who it could be banging at this time of night. I reached for my service weapon and got out of bed. I wasn't afraid but I definitely wanted to be cautious.

I hadn't raised the gun yet. I called out as I headed to the door. "Who is it?"

"It's me," said the voice on the other end of the phone. I felt the chill go through my body as I heard his voice. I put my gun down on the table by the front door and threw it open.

I reached out my hand and grabbed him by the t-shirt to pull him in. He kicked the door closed behind him as we started to kiss. Young's big hands gripped at my ass as our lips said everything we hadn't said. We didn't need any words yet.

It felt so good to be kissing my man again. I knew that it had only been a week but it felt like forever since I'd seen him. It felt so good to be touching him instead of dreaming about him, even if the dream had felt real.

"I missed you so much," I finally said with a

huff after a couple of minutes. I didn't know, or care how long we'd been kissing. I just needed to tell him that. He didn't say anything, his lips said it all with more kisses.

Young didn't need to say anything to me. His actions said it all. His tall frame got down on both knees. His face came right up to my stomach. He started to lick and kiss all over it. He planted soft kisses all over my abdomen, getting lower and lower as he slowly removed all of my clothes, right there by the front door.

Once my clothes were off though, it seemed like Young was done with the soft stuff. He laid me on the floor. My back felt cold against the hardwood but I didn't mind it at all. Young was keeping me plenty warm. He grabbed me by my waist and positioned my body so that he could lower himself down onto me face first.

Young's tongue was long and wet as he started eating me out. I was squirming on the floor as he entered me. His powerful hands were gripping my body tightly as I half fought to get away. It was feeling amazing. I could feel the stubble on his face rubbing against my thighs.

"Damn," Young said. He sounded out of

breath like he was only just coming up for air. "You taste better than I remember."

I opened my mouth to speak but only a moan came out. I put my hand on the back of his head and gently guided his head back down where it needed to be. It didn't take much work because Young seemed to be getting as much pleasure from it as I was.

He kept on eating me out for a couple more minutes and my body exploded with a powerful orgasm soon afterwards. It was his turn next and I was more than happy to help him get off the same way that he'd done for me.

I thought about just climbing onto him and riding him like there was no tomorrow but I decided to indulge in some foreplay first.

I grabbed his head with both of my hands and pulled him out from between my legs. His face looked funny because it was practically shining with all of my juices all over him. The look on his face almost made me laugh because he looked like a kid who'd been caught with his hand in the cookie jar.

"What?" He asked.

"Nothing," I said with a smirk. "Just turn over."

He got a devilish look on his face. "Aight," he said. He sat up and turned over. Once he was sitting up he removed the rest of his clothes and then laid back on the floor slowly.

I got up and straddled him. My nipples rubbed against his when I leaned down to kiss him. I could taste myself on his lips but I didn't mind it one bit. I turned Young's head to the side and slowly started to lick on his neck with the tip of my tongue. After a while the gentle licking turned to kissing and then sucking.

"Fuck!" Young said with a grunt.

I was moving across his body with a mission. I knew the ways to turn a man on and I was putting in a lot of work on Young. I moved from one side of his neck to the other, licking and sucking as I went. I would move down his nipples and lick on those too. I knew that most guys tried to act like they didn't like all of this stuff but behind closed doors they loved it. Young was rock hard and I'd barely done anything to his dick.

Moving my body down his, I was face to face with his dick. I was looking at it and thinking about how much I missed it. It had only been about a week or so but it felt like forever. I reached out and grabbed it in my hand, jerking it a little bit.

I eased my mouth onto it slowly. I didn't want to rush any part of it. I bobbed my head up and down slowly in an effort to build a rhythm. I wanted it to feel good to him. It only took a little while to know that I was doing the right thing.

Young's head looked down at me a couple of times as I was giving him head. It was like he couldn't believe how good it felt. He put his hand on the back of my head and started to push me down onto his dick. I didn't mind it. In fact, when he applied more pressure, I went with it. I deep throated him and all that.

I finally thought he was on the verge of coming so I stopped. It was right on time too. The look that he gave me when I was finished was enough to let me know that I could expect something good to happen next.

Once Young had slipped a condom onto himself, that was it. I was laying on my back and he was on top of me going in! We started off in the missionary position which I've always been a big fan of because I love kissing.

Young put his hands on my waist and lifted

me off the floor a little bit so he could really dig me out. I reached up onto the couch and grabbed a pillow, putting it beneath my head. Young had worked up a thin layer of sweat that was making his skin glisten. His dick felt good as it worked itself in and out of me. I was also getting turned on by watching his muscles flex and move as he worked himself in and out of me. The only sounds to be heard were from out money and his body slapping against mine.

Young and I finished up a couple of minutes later. At least, that was the first time. After doing it right there in front of the front door, we headed into the actual living room and my baby hit it from the back on the couch. I'd never been a sex fiend or anything like that. I liked it of course, but it wasn't until I'd gotten with Young that I felt like was becoming dick hungry. It was like I just couldn't get enough of him. The two of us spent hours having sex all over my apartment before finally ending up on my bed, exhausted.

"I feel like I'm dehydrated now," Young said goofily. He dramatically wiped his forehead like there was sweat there or something.

"You're not the only one. I thought we were

both gonna pass out that last time.," I said with a little laugh. I was laying on my back and Young was lying next to me. We weren't touching one another. It wasn't intentional. It got kind of quiet and I think it was the awkwardness of the situation setting in. We hadn't really said much to one another, at least not with words.

"I'm sorry for going ghost on you," Young said as he rolled over closer to me and extended one of his long arms over my body. "I'm sorry about everything. I shouldn't have left you in Miami like that. I had some business to take care of but I could have done you better than that."

Young was of course being vague about what business he had flown back to take care of. Of course he didn't know that Officer Harris had already told me all about it. I wasn't about to let him in on that though. I felt the need to keep my secrets close, if only because he did the same.

"I know, but..." I trailed off. I didn't have to say anything about it. Young picked up on what I hadn't said and pulled me in a little closer to him. I didn't want to have to be one of those chicks who had to get all in their man's face and stuff like that. Young knew he fucked up but I wanted him to know that saying sorry wasn't enough, even on top of the sex.

"I'm sorry," he said again. He sounded just as sincere as he did the first time around. He kissed me on the neck a few times. "I just need you to hold it down for a little while longer and then we gonna be back how we were before," he said. "It's crazy out here for me and I wanna tell you about it but all in due time."

"You promise?" I asked. I looked him in the eyes so he knew how serious I was being.

"Yeah," he said with a nod. "No bullshit."

I smiled at him and nodded my head.

Young and I cuddled close to one another and drifted off to sleep. It felt so good to be lying in bed with him. I felt so much of the bullshit of the week that we hadn't been speaking fall away. It was hard to hold on to all of that stuff when Young was finally back where he belonged, right with me.

I woke up a couple of hours later before my alarm went off. The instant that I was awake, I realized that I was alone again. I must've been in a deep sleep because I didn't even feel or hear

Young get up and go. I thought for sure that I would have heard the door close or something. I started crying again.

My emotions were all out of balance. I was a mess and I decided that instead of trying to pull it together, I could just stay home and take some time to deal. I called in to work and let them know that I wouldn't be coming in. I gave the operator an excuse about me being sick but she didn't really care.

I thought about why I was crying again and I realized that the truth of the matter was that I was really just upset because I hadn't been able to spend time with Young the way that I wanted to. It had only been two or three hours. I loved the feeling of him being inside of me and even when we finished having sex, his arms around me made me feel safe. It felt good to know that he was safe, too.

CHAPTER 8

MAKING the decision not to go to work seemed like it was going to be the best thing that I'd done in a while. Since I wasn't going to work, I decided to do stuff that I didn't normally do. I hadn't cooked anything in a while so I decided to start my day off with something I hadn't had in a while: a home cooked meal. The more I thought about it, the more I realized that staying home and making myself some breakfast might be just the thing I was looking for to help me out of my rut. I knew it was bad that I was in my feelings because Young wasn't around but it was something I just needed to deal with.

I put on some shorts and a tank top and slipped my slippers on my feet. Opening the door to my bedroom I thought I heard some noise coming from the living room. It sounded like someone snoring but I *knew* that it couldn't have been that. Young had left. He wasn't in my bed. I didn't get up to check but if he had stayed, he would have come back to bed. I knew that for sure. The nose made me a little tense as I walked to the living room.

I headed to the couch and sure enough, Young was right there sprawled out. He was asleep. My baby looked like an angel when he slept. His hand was down the front of his underwear. I had never been able to figure out why guys did that when they went to sleep.

I sat down on the couch and nudged him a little bit. His eyes opened up slowly and he looked at me.

"Yo, what are you doing here? I thought you left," I said to him. I was still confused.

"Nah," he said with a yawn as he sat up a little, "nah, I stayed."

"Duh, fool. I can see that," I said. "What happened though? Why are you out here? Why you ain't come back to bed?"

"After we chilled, we both fell asleep and when I got up to leave it was too late," he said it like it was the most simple thing in the world.

"What does that even mean?" I asked. I was confused still. "Why couldn't you just leave?" It wasn't like I didn't want him around or anything like that. I was just trying to figure out the situation.

"I'm not tryin' to be seen," he said. "I gotta move on the low and you never know who's watching. I be on my vampire shit, only out when it's no sunlight. So if it's cool with you, can I chill out here until later on?"

I just started smiling like crazy. "Yeah, it's cool, you don't even have to ask. Feel free to stay as long as you need to. It's funny cause I called out of work today. I woke up and wasn't feeling too good. I had a headache."

"Oh word?" he asked as he sat up a little more. He smirked. "How convenient? So you just gonna be in here with me today?"

"Yup," I said as I pecked him on the lips.

"So, what you wanna do today? It's just gonna be us," Young said.

"I was just about to make breakfast. I got enough for two people though," I replied.

"Let me cook," he said. I was looking at him

for any traces of a smile but he had a dead serious look on his face.

"You?" I asked. I didn't know if Young could cook or not but I'd just assumed that he couldn't.

"Yeah," he said with a nod. "I can cook," he said defensively.

"I'll be the judge of that," I said playfully.

"What's in there to make?" he asked me as he stood up.

"Umm, I have some eggs, bacon, sausage, bread, whatever you want. I went food shopping not too long ago so it's fully stocked," I said.

"Aight, cool," he said. Young got up and headed into the kitchen. I stood up and walked over to the kitchen and sat on the other side of the island on one of the stools.

"What you doing?" Young asked me. He'd found the pots and had a frying pan in his hand, about to place it on the stove.

"Sitting here," I said. "What you mean?"

"Nah," he said as he shook his head, "this ain't the cooking channel. If you want a show, go watch that. You gonna mess me up." He had a smile on his face but I could tell that he was still serious too.

"Oh my gosh," I said playfully, "I can't believe this. I'm getting kicked out of my own kitchen."

"You'll be aight," he said. "Let me do my thing."

About twenty minutes later, Young had definitely done his thing. French Toast and omelets were on the menu.

Young brought the food out to me and put my plate on the coffee table in front of me. He grabbed his and brought out two glasses of water with lemon. I snapped a picture of the food with my phone because it looked that good. He'd sprinkled powdered sugar on top of the toast and the omelet looked soft and fluffy.

"Damn, this looks good," I gushed over the food. I couldn't wait to eat it.

"And it tastes good too," Young said. I was definitely surprised that he could cook. I tasted the food and everything that he'd said was true; the food was amazing. I loved it.

Young cooking breakfast for me was just the start of what turned out to be a regular day. With him not going anywhere until later on and me having called out of work, the two of us just chilled and vibed with one another. It was like that week where we hadn't seen one another hadn't just happened.

Spending the day with him only made me fall more in love with him. We sat on the couch and watched daytime TV. Well, I watched a lot of the gossip shows and he dealt with it for a little bit until he asked me to turn on ESPN.

We made love a couple of times. We'd gotten in the shower with each other and did it in there right after breakfast. We got out and oiled each other up and then ended up fucking again. We just couldn't get enough of one another.

It was like the outside world wasn't there. He did get a couple of texts and a phone call or two but nothing major. Whoever it was couldn't have been that important because he didn't talk to them for too long or get into long text conversations with them. I liked that he was trying hard to be present and just spend time with me.

"Hmmm," I thought, "what's your dream vacation?" Young and I were sitting on my couch again, halfway paying attention to the TV. We'd put a movie on but it was one that we'd both seen a thousand times before it was cool not to watch.

"Where'd that come from?" Young asked. I was sitting up and he was laying with his head resting on my lap as I rubbed his head.

"The movie, fool," I said with a laugh. "They're about to get rich. The first thing I'd do is go on vacation if I had money."

"Where would you go?" Young asked. I really appreciated the fact that he was listening to me so intently. Our day together hadn't been scheduled or anything like that but it seemed to be working out in our favor. Young and I were getting closer and taking some much needed time to get to know each other better. It felt like we were making up for the time we lost in Miami.

"I asked you first," I said.

"So," he smirked, "I'm asking *you* now."

I playfully rolled my eyes at him. "I'd go to Switzerland," I said without hesitation.

"Word? Why there?" He asked. I was glad that he hadn't made fun of me the way that a lot of other people might of when I said that. I knew that it probably wasn't the first place that people thought of when it came to dream vacations but I had my reasons.

"I watch the Travel Channel a lot, like *a lot*,"

I emphasized. "I've always been a fan of other cultures and stuff like that. I just think it's cool how we can all be so different in so many ways. Anyway, I saw a documentary about the city of Zurich and it made me add it to the top of my bucket list. It's a beautiful city and there's so much culture there."

"I wanna see that documentary. It sounds like something I'd like," he said. "I think it's so cool that you're into shit like that. I done been around a lot of women and none of them got what you got, that's why I like you. I wanna take you to Zurich. I wanna help you live out that dream and all the others that you have if you'll let me."

Young was being sincere and it was only making me fall deeper and deeper in love with him. "I'd like that a lot," I said. I bent my head down and kissed him. "What's on your mind?"

"Nothing really," he said as he stifled a yawn. "I think I got an answer to your question though."

"Oh, really? What is it?" I asked.

"I think I'd wanna go to the South of France, like Saint-Tropez," he said. "I've seen a lot of pictures of it and it just seems like a place

I'd like to visit. It's popular but private and I seen the beaches out there and they look like something you'd only see in movies. I wanna take you there too."

Young and I enjoyed our time together, but as the day went on, I was reminded about the fact that once nighttime came, he was going to take off again and I wouldn't be hearing from him until all of this stuff with the rival gang blew over. He didn't know that I knew that part though. I tried not to let it to get to me but it was constantly in the back of my mind.

Young and I spent real quality time with one another that day. As much as I didn't want it to come, the end of the day was soon upon us. The afternoon passed in what felt like a blur and before we knew it, the gun was going down and giving him the cover of night that he'd been waiting for. Earlier in the day I toyed with the idea of asking him if it was possible for him to stay a little longer. I would have loved it if it were possible but I didn't even ask. Earlier in the day he made it clear that once it was dark enough that was his cue to leave and head to wherever he went when he wasn't with me.

Young and I stood facing one another in

front of my door. He'd showered and was fully dressed in front of me about to leave again. At least he'd able to give me a real goodbye this time around.

"You got everything?" I asked him.

"Yeah," he replied. He was different now. I didn't know what it was but it felt like he was more stressed now. I think being inside the house with me all day had been just the break that he needed. I knew that he had to be stressing out because of the stuff he had going on so it was probably good for him to have taken a day away from it.

"I hope you enjoyed yourself," I said to him. I told myself that I wasn't going to get emotional and I'd meant it. I knew that Young was safe and that if anything happened, I'd hear about it one way or another. To keep my own sanity, I knew that I needed to not worry about him.

"Of course," Young said. "You gonna be good?" he asked me. I knew that his question was asking more about me in a general sense.

"Yeah," I said. "Just hit me up if you can."

"I'll try," Young said. He leaned down and kissed me on the lips. I wrapped my arms around him and held on to him for a while before finally letting him go.

"I'll see you later," Young said before he unlocked the door and stepped out. I closed and locked the door behind him.

CHAPTER 9

A BITCH WAS *BUZZING* as I walked into work the next morning. I was full of energy and in a great mood that I definitely wasn't about to let anyone mess up for me. Taking off the day before had really been exactly what I needed to set me back on the right track. I'd slept a lot so I was rejuvenated, not to mention that all of the sex that Young and I had was definitely a mood booster.

My fellow officers seemed to pick up on my mood too. I'd gotten to work early so I was taking my time getting dressed. I was making small talk with some of the other ladies. There was some new movie coming out with Morris Chestnut and a bunch of them were gushing over him. He was handsome, but a little too old for me. I chimed in every now and then though.

I was trying to put my best foot forward. It might not have shown but I'd been distracted lately. I was hoping that since I'd seen Young, I'd be able to focus. I didn't want to have any more slip ups and I definitely wanted to make sure that my head was where it was supposed to be.

After I finished getting dressed I headed towards the briefing room. It wasn't full but there were a decent amount of people inside. I saw Officer Harris on the other side of the room. I nodded in his direction and he nodded back at me. No need to make it a big thing.

I spotted Officer Briggs seated towards the front. It looked like he'd been saving the seat next to him for me. I walked up behind him and patted him on the shoulder as I sat down.

"How you doing this morning?" I asked him.

"I'm alright," he said with a yawn. He'd been a little tired lately.

"You been getting enough sleep?" I asked him. "You've been a little out of it on patrol lately."

"I've just been a little tired," he said. "You

know my wife's pregnant. This one is kicking her ass so when she's up sick, I'm up taking care of her."

I didn't even want to think about being pregnant, not after my scare with Young. I couldn't imagine my life being changed in that way, at least not so early on. "It'll be over soon enough," I said. "She's due in a couple of weeks."

Briggs laughed. "Oh please. I get to trade a sick wife in for a crying baby. I'm *definitely* not getting any sleep. That's why I have this," he said as he held up his coffee cup and kissed it.

"How was yesterday?" I asked him. I was a responsible person so I hated calling out of work, even if it is justified.

"It was pretty quiet," he said. "You'll be happy to hear that I got through a shit ton of paperwork too."

I raised my eyebrows and gave him a mini round of applause. Briggs made it clear that he hated paperwork and would rather not do it but he didn't want to put all of it on me so he helped out from time to time. "Wow, I'm glad you were able to take care of yourself without me around. No paper cuts?" I playfully asked him.

"I'm the FTO, remember?" he joked back. I loved the dynamic that I had with Briggs. He was just so cool that it made it easy to talk to him.

"The bosses are here," I said as I turned and spotted a group of people walking in busily. I hated the way that they tried to make themselves look more important by always arriving just as the meeting was starting.

I always paid attention in the briefings because I never wanted to miss out on any information. On that particular day I was definitely paying attention.

The Sergeant connected his computer to the projector and an image of Young and some other dude were projected on the screen. I felt my stomach sink. I hoped nothing happened to him. I was tense but I needed to act as normal as possible.

"Here we have two familiar faces," the Sergeant began, "Eric Mayfield, also known as Young, leader of the notorious gang, the AB Boys. On the right we have Kevin "Fast"

Ambrose, leader of the GMG or Get Money Gang.

"Now, these two have been in our crosshairs for multiple reasons over the years. Each of them has their hands in a whole bunch of shady shit: drugs, murder, credit scams, the works. The problem has always been that they've both been careful. We've gotten small players but nothing has ever been able to stick to either of them," the Sergeant said.

I was hanging onto his every word. I wondered where his speech was going.

"There is apparently honor among thieves because as far as we know, these two have always avoided one another. They've stayed out of each other's hair until now. For some reason, the GMG have been going after AB boy territory in a big way and now the rival gangs are locked in a war. We believe that this could be our chance to nail one or both of them. A war means more bodies and more action on the street. We need everyone to keep their eyes open and their ears clean. There's gonna be blood on the street from this one," he said.

The sergeant went on, telling us about what we should be on the lookout for. I listened to what he said but I also began to wonder about how they knew about the war between the two gangs. Young didn't know that I knew about it and he definitely didn't know that the NYPD knew about it. He thought that he'd been moving in silence but somehow people had found out.

I knew that I was probably just being dumb about it but I wondered if him staying with me had done more harm than good. Maybe that was how he'd slipped up and didn't even realize it.

I thought about it for a little while and was on the verge of telling Young about it. I knew that I wasn't supposed to hit him up until all of this blew over but he had a right to know. I went back and forth about it for the rest of the briefing but ultimately decided against it. Officer Harris would probably end up telling Young himself. I was already involved with him enough. I needed to think long and hard before I decided to get that involved in Young's *other* life, especially since he didn't try and include me in it himself.

After the briefing was over, Briggs and I headed to inspect our patrol car before we headed out for the day. Once we saw that every-thing was fine, we headed out in patrol.

"I've been thinking about leaving the force," Briggs said. We'd been quiet for a last few minutes, reaching a lull in our conversation. He was driving so I turned and looked at him. I hadn't been expecting him to say that at all.

"What makes you wanna do that?" I asked him. Briggs and I were still feeling one another out. I knew that him admitting something like this to me had to mean that we were getting closer. I liked Briggs and wanted to get to know him better.

"Well, my wife is pregnant again and I can already see how it's affecting us. With two kids, she's gonna need more help around the house. She doesn't want to be a stay at home mom and she shouldn't have to be either. I've been thinking about getting into a different line of work; something safer and something that'll let me be around more," he explained.

"That makes sense," I said. Briggs and I were in two totally different situations but I could relate to his feelings about safety. When-ever I did have a family, I knew that I didn't want to still be working on the force. "You have to do what's best for your family. What does your wife think of it?"

"She supports it. She just wants to make sure that I'm happy and that we have insurance. Kids are expensive. Don't have any," Briggs joked. He didn't know how close to home he was hitting after my pregnancy scare from a few weeks ago.

"Have you guys thought about names yet?" I asked.

"No, not yet," he said. "We've thrown around a couple of them but I think we both would just rather see her and come up with a name."

"Well, Taela is a great name," I joked. Briggs joined in on my laughter.

"Come in, this is dispatch. We've got a report of drunk and disorderly behavior," came the voice over the radio. "Are you available? Over."

The call had come from a couple of blocks away. We got the address and Briggs took off headed in the direction.

When we got there, there was a woman who appeared to be homeless standing on the corner. She was heckling people for money in an aggressive way, walking alongside people, getting in their faces, the works.

I surveyed the situation and decided that I could handle it. "I think I got this one," I told Briggs. "You can hang back and play support." The woman looked like she was in her early 50s or so. I didn't think she'd be much of an issue.

"Sounds like a plan," Briggs said. I was glad that he hadn't questioned me on it.

I got out of the car and calmly walked up to the woman. Briggs hung back close to the car. The woman was wearing an old pair of black jeans that were beat up but at least didn't have any holes in them. Her hair was pulled back into a ponytail. It was mostly gray but you could tell that it used to be black. She didn't look too bad but the look in her eyes let me know that she was a little drunk.

"Ma'am, we got a call about someone being drunk and disorderly. Is there somewhere we can take you? If not, we need you to keep it moving down the street," I said. I kept my voice calm but was still firm.

"What the fuck do you want?" the woman asked. She wasn't yelling but she was definitely louder than necessary. "Fucking cops always bothering me and shit." I didn't know if she was talking more to me or herself.

"Ma'am, I'm not trying to bother you. Some people reported being harassed," I said. I was trying to reason with her. There wasn't' a need to turn it into a bigger thing. I was expecting some big scene, not a harmless old woman.

"I wasn't bothering nobody," the woman said. "That bitch...that bitch," she mumbled.

"Who the fuck you callin' a bitch?" A voice came from behind me. My back had been turned so I didn't even realize that another homeless woman had walked up behind me. She wasn't helping the situation at all and only seemed to be antagonizing the situation.

"Ma'am, please," I said to the woman who'd just walked up. The first woman was drinking so who know what could have happened.

"She always callin' me out my name like she better than me. That bitch ain't better than nobody," the second woman said.

"Fuck you!" the drunk woman yelled as she tried to lunge at the second. The problem was that I was standing in the middle of the two of them. The drunk woman had her arms out and was grabbing at the other woman. I tried to use my elbow to separate them but they were clawing at one another too much.

Everything happened so fast that I didn't even see Briggs come over. He'd grabbed the drunk woman up. I regained my composure and grabbed the second woman by her shirt, backing her into a corner.

"What the fuck? She started it," the woman said.

"You instigated it," I said to her.

Getting caught up in a fight between two old woman wasn't my ideal day but it had served as a reminder of something. It was good to have Briggs by my side. He was a good partner and someone that I could trust. Twice now I've found myself in situations that could have gone completely wrong if not for him watching my back.

CHAPTER 10

AFTER ALL THE craziness of the day before, I was glad for the relative calmness that Briggs and I had seen so far the next day. We ended up taking in both of the homeless women because they wouldn't calm down. We'd kept them separated but they just wanted to claw at one another and kept trying to treat Briggs and I like we were doing something wrong by trying to stop them. It was especially annoying because it didn't have to get that far. I was sure that they were probably both about to be out soon enough, we'd only taken them in for drunk and disorderly conduct, nothing crazy.

The entire morning had been quiet, almost too quiet. We hadn't gotten calls for anything major and everything in our patrol area was fine. We were keeping our eyes and ears peeled but it seemed to be pretty chill for the most part. Briggs and I even went to a diner and sat down for lunch instead of grabbing something and eating it in a hurry in the car.

"Kinda weird, isn't it?" I asked as I drove down the street.

"What?" Briggs asked. He'd been gazing out the window not really paying attention.

"It's so quiet today," I said. I'd been thinking it for a while.

"Kinda nice you mean?" Briggs shook his head. "You know you're not supposed to say shit like that out loud. Something's gonna happen now," he said. He was half joking and half serious. "This could just be the calm before the storm."

"Let's hope not. We've only got two more hours out here before we can call it a day," I said. The day had been fine but it was still work. I was in the mood to get home. I'd bought a bottle of white wine and it was sitting in the fridge waiting for me. I was gonna curl up with it and watch a nice movie.

We kept on patrolling for a few more

minutes, making small talk. Briggs must have been a psychic because I'd definitely jinxed it. The familiar crackling of the staticky radio came on. "Car 2048, come in please. We've gotten a report of suspected gang activity close to your sector and would like you to check it out. Over."

I grabbed the radio. "Copy that. Send the address and we'll check it out. Over."

Dispatch sent the location over. They told us to keep a lookout over the area which was a couple of square blocks but told us to pay attention to one block in particular. I drove us up and down a couple of blocks, keeping an eye out for anything. It was pretty quiet. I pulled up on the corner of the block they wanted us to check out.

"If anything happens, I'm telling my wife to blame you for jinxing us," Briggs said with a laugh as he stepped out of the car. I climbed out on my side as well. The street that we were on was a quiet one. It was full of brownstones, but they were old and in the process of being repaired. The sun was shining but half of the street was darkened by scaffolding. There were a couple of people walking past but it looked quiet for the most part.

"Oh please," I said. "It's been quiet all day."

"And it better stay that way. Let's just walk it and see if we see anybody in these alleys," he said.

We started walking up the right side of the street. An old woman eyed us. Our eyes met and she rolled hers at me. I swear, I'd never get used to the polarizing views that I got for putting on this uniform. Some people loved it, others hated it. To some people I was a hero and to others a sellout. The thing was, it was my job to protect them all.

Briggs and I walked up the block slowly. Everything was fine and there didn't seem to be anything wrong. I couldn't help but to wonder again how it was that my unit knew what was going on. I wasn't a detective so there was obviously a lot of information that I wasn't privy to, but I couldn't figure out how they seemed to know so much. Young made it seem like he'd been really careful with everything that he did and no one really knew he was in New York according to Officer Harris.

"Pussy!" someone yelled. The sound was coming from behind one of the brownstones ahead of us. I didn't know which one. I didn't know whose voice it was but they sounded pissed off. I stopped walking and locked eyes with Briggs. The voice deep as hell so we knew it had to belong to a man.

"Think we should check it out?" I asked. Briggs was still the FTO and as a result of that, I thought it best to just follow his judgement calls. I wanted to be cautious about the situation.

"Nah, might be noth—" Briggs was cut off by someone yelling from the same place.

"Fuck you nigga!" The voice boomed. It sounded like it was closer than the other one was. I felt my stomach drop and I almost lost my balance just standing there. I didn't know who the first person yelling was but I knew that second voice for sure, I'd heard it all day yesterday. I didn't know why Young was there but I was sure I was about to find out.

"Yo!" Young's voice yelled. It sounded like relief, like he was signaling for someone.

Briggs and I were making our way up the block by that point. We didn't know what was happening but we're damn sure wanted to know. We didn't say anything as we quickly walked.

Boom! Boom! Boom!

The gunshots rang out quickly, one after another. Instinctively, I dropped to the ground and reached for my weapon. Briggs did the same. The two of us locked eyes and as another two shots rang out from behind a brownstone close to where we were, he tipped his head to the side to indicate that we should head behind a parked car on the street.

I was sure that the majority of the shooting was coming from behind the house but that didn't make me feel any safer. My heart was pounding but I kept my head down as I quickly scurried behind the car. Briggs came over right behind me. The two of us rested our backs against the car, breathing hard and trying to catch our breath. Shit had gone from calm to crazy in no time flat.

"What the fuck is happening back there?" I asked. I wasn't panicked but I was pumping nothing but adrenaline through my veins. This was a lot more than I'd bargained for but I knew it was all a part of the job.

"I think it's a fucking turf war. I saw a bunch of people shooting at each other," he said. We both ducked our heads down as more shots rang out. I could hear the sounds of people yelling and glass shattering as it got hit.

"Dispatch! Come in dispatch. Shots fired! I repeat, shots fired! We are pinned down and need back up," Briggs yelled into his radio. Dispatch came through quickly letting us know that people were on the way but the closest car was a couple of blocks away.

"Fuck!" I yelled out loud. "What are we gonna do?" I wasn't really asking Briggs. I just needed to think out loud before I went crazy.

"Our car is down the block but we don't have a clear shot at it. I think the shooting is moving this way. We might get past this first alley but the second one is more open and that was where the shooting was coming from," Briggs said quickly. I guess being a FTO meant something because he was still training me, even in this real life situation.

I listened between the gunshots, trying to pin down where the shooting was coming from or how many people there were. It was hard to tell because it all sounded like noise to me.

Briggs turned around and got into a crouching position. I wanted to ask him what the hell he thought he was doing but before I could, he unlatched his gun and pulled it out. He stood up, pointed and started shooting towards the alley where the shooting was coming from. He fired off two rounds before ducking back down.

I didn't say anything to him. I was wondering if that was a smart move but I decided not to question it. Briggs had been doing this longer and was more experienced than I was. Not to mention that he'd been getting me out of trouble the entire time that we'd been partners. The other cars were closer. I could hear their sirens getting louder. I wondered if Young was still out there, if that had been him. I knew his voice but I was hoping it wasn't really him.

Briggs stood up again, this time for a little longer. He fired off another two rounds before ducking back down next to me. He was free to do that but I was on the lookout for a *smart* way to shoot. I'd peered up through the broken glass and saw that there were a lot of them. I couldn't really tell who was fighting for which side though.

I turned around and crouched. I'd already pulled out my weapon a while ago. I clenched it tightly in my hand, the metal warm from my grip. I peered around the car, trying to get a clear view of anything. I needed to improve my view so that I knew where or if I should even be shooting.

A figure darted past the back, running from the front of one building to the next. It was obviously a male, and a very tall one at that. It had to be Young, I hoped. I was pretty sure that I had recognized his voice earlier. He sped passed me quickly but I knew it had to be him.

I was still crouched and looking down the block on both sides, hoping to see backup come. Briggs was still crouched and his head was moving rapidly looking for a chance to shoot. He finally must've seen it. He stood up quickly and fired off two shots.

"Get down!" I yelled to Briggs. He'd been standing up for a couple of seconds too long. He was risking exposing himself.

More shots rang out I knew immediately that something had gone wrong. Briggs didn't fall back. He stumbled back onto one leg and halfway fell onto the ground with a thump as he tried to catch himself. His hands grabbed at his abdomen.

"I'm hit," Briggs announced.

Find out what happens next in part three of Cuffed To A Savage! Available Now!

To find out when Mia Black has new books available, **follow Mia Black on Instagram: @authormiablack**

CUFFED TO A SAVAGE 3

Tae and her partner, Officer Briggs, have just taken fire, but that's not the worst that has happened. While Officer Briggs lays dying, she wrestles with the harsh reality of his devastating injuries and what it will do to her comrades and the horrible truth that Young, her secret lover, may be involved.

Forced to choose between the man she loves and the oath she took when she joined the force, Tae faces a crisis of morality and a deeply personal crisis about her own life and how much it will change with or without Young's freedom.

Find out what happens next in part three of Cuffed To A Savage! Available Now!

To find out when Mia Black has new books available, **follow Mia Black on Instagram: @authormiablack**

Made in the USA
Middletown, DE
11 December 2021

55200319R00076